MURDER, SHE SAID

'If you want to discuss murder,' said Raymond, 'you must talk to my Aunt Jane.'

———— ◆ ————

'Greenshaw's Folly'

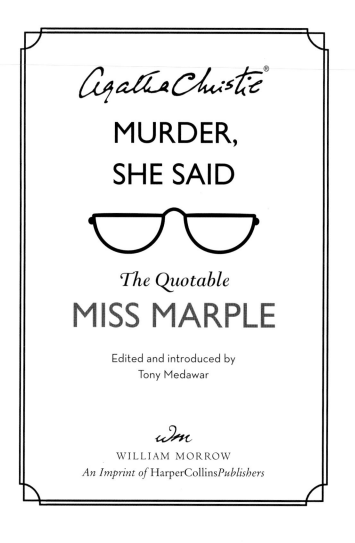

Agatha Christie®

MURDER,
SHE SAID

The Quotable
MISS MARPLE

Edited and introduced by
Tony Medawar

WILLIAM MORROW
An Imprint of HarperCollinsPublishers

MURDER, SHE SAID. Copyright © Agatha Christie Limited 2019. All rights reserved. Printed in China. No part of this book may be used or reproduced in any manner whatsoever without written permission except in the case of brief quotations embodied in critical articles and reviews. For information, address HarperCollins Publishers, 195 Broadway, New York, NY 10007.

HarperCollins books may be purchased for educational, business, or sales promotional use. For information, please email the Special Markets Department at SPsales@harpercollins.com.

FIRST EDITION

Library of Congress Cataloging-in-Publication Data has been applied for.

ISBN 978-0-06-296837-1

19 20 21 22 23   10 9 8 7 6 5 4 3 2 1

CONTENTS

INTRODUCING
MISS JANE MARPLE

'Miss Marple was not in any way a picture of my grandmother; she was far more fussy and spinsterish than my grandmother ever was. But one thing she did have in common with her – though a cheerful person, she always expected the worst of everyone and everything, and was, with almost frightening accuracy, usually proved right.'

Agatha Christie
An Autobiography

Agatha Christie's *other* great detective, Miss Jane Marple, first appeared in December 1927 in a series of short stories published in the *Royal* magazine.

Christie herself suggested that Miss Marple should be seen as a shrewder version of Caroline Sheppard, a woman whose brother helped a certain retired Belgian police officer to investigate *The Murder of Roger Ackroyd* (1926). Miss Sheppard had been Agatha Christie's *'favourite character in the book – an acidulated spinster full of curiosity, knowing everything, hearing everything: the complete detective service in the home'*, someone in fact very much like the friends of Agatha Christie's much loved step-grandmother, 'Auntie-Granny' Margaret Miller, whose influence can also be detected in the character of Miss Marple.

In the first story in which she appears, 'The Tuesday Night Club', Miss Marple is discovered 'at home' in Danemead, her house in the pretty village of St Mary Mead. She is sitting erect by the hearth in a room with broad black beams across the ceiling, furnished with *good old furniture that belonged to it*. She is knitting and wearing '*a black brocade dress, very much pinched in around the waist. Mechlin lace was arranged in a cascade down the front of the bodice. She had on black mittens, and a black lace cap surmounted the piled-up masses of her snowy hair*'. Tonight she has a visitor, the writer Raymond West who is her favourite nephew, and this evening they are entertaining some of Raymond's friends. Miss Marple almost passes unnoticed in the group's discussion of one unsolved mystery after another until in each case she, and she alone, points unerringly to the truth by applying the insights into human nature that she has gained from a lifetime of observation.

'An old lady with a sweet, placid spinsterish face, and a mind that has plumbed the depths of human iniquity.'
Sir Henry Clithering, *The Body in the Library*

Although the precise date of her birth would seem to be unknowable, there are several glimpses of Miss Marple's early life in the twelve novels and twenty short stories in which she appears.

We know that Jane Marple was born in the second half of the nineteenth century and that, with her sister, she was home-schooled by Miss Ledbury and other governesses. When she was a little older, Jane was sent to a boarding school in Florence where she learned French and, with her hair in pigtails, she was taught decimals and English literature by a German governess.

Although Jane appears to have had only the one sibling, she came from a very large family and in the stories there are fleeting references to her mother and her grandmother as well as various cousins and countless aunts and uncles, great aunts and great uncles, nieces, nephews and godchildren. And while she never married, there were certainly men in her life, such as a young man she met at a croquet party who had seemed eligible but turned out to be very, very dull. Jane was anything but dull. She enjoyed dancing, opera at Covent Garden and the theatre.

Jane was not without a sense of the theatrical herself. She had a fondness for practical trickery and a talent for mimicry which would one day save someone's life. She read widely, including books by Jerome K. Jerome and, as an adult, those of Dashiell Hammett. She enjoyed poetry and could quote from Swinburne and Shakespeare as well as from the Bible, which she would sometimes misquote for her own amusement. Jane appreciated art, particularly the art of the magician, and enjoyed conjuring tricks, cinema and Madame Tussaud's, the wax museum in London.

As a child, Jane very much enjoyed going shopping at the Army & Navy Store in Victoria with her Aunt Helen, whose husband was Canon of Ely Cathedral, and she sometimes stayed with another uncle who was Canon of Chichester Cathedral. Clearly, hers was a very Christian family and, when she was a child, a biblical homily was pinned above her bed – 'Ask and you shall receive'. It was a text Jane Marple would keep in mind throughout her life: if she was in trouble, she would say a little prayer and she maintained that she always received an answer. She believed in eternal life and kept by her bedside a copy of *The Imitation of Christ*, a devotional volume by Thomas à Kempis.

> 'She's had a long life of experience in evil,
> in noticing evil, fancying evil, suspecting evil and
> going forth to do battle with evil.'
> Chief Inspector Fred Davy, *At Bertram's Hotel*

Significantly, given her later commitment to rooting out evil, Jane Marple never had any doubt that those who commit the severest of crimes should receive the severest of punishments and she was more than ready herself to be ruthless in the cause of justice, even to the extent of setting traps and lying.

Though she was raised in a city, Miss Marple spent most of her life in the country, in the village of St Mary Mead, which her nephew regarded as *'the kind of village where nothing ever happens. Exactly like a stagnant pond'*, a comment that earned a stern rebuke from his aunt: *'Nothing, I believe, is so full of life under the microscope as a drop of water from a stagnant pool'*. The name of St Mary Mead, along with those of other towns and geographical features, suggest that the village is somewhere on the border of West Sussex and Hampshire though Dr Marty S. Knepper has suggested that when Agatha Christie created the village she was in fact thinking of Sunningdale in Berkshire.

Miss Marple went to church on Sundays and she was well-known at all levels of society in the village, from the village policeman and the barmaid at The Blue Boar pub to the chief constable of the county and the vicar by whom she was regularly invited for Christmas dinner.

While life in St Mary Mead presented some frustrations for Miss Marple, not least the haphazard performance of domestic servants and the inability to buy proper glass cloths and good quality household linen, she loved it for the opportunities it provided to examine the human condition. '*So many interesting human problems – giving rise to endless pleasurable hours of speculation …*'

Throughout her life when pondering more serious problems she would often identify a village parallel, such as the mysterious disappearance of two gills of pickled shrimps or the curious instance of the gardener who worked on a bank holiday.

However, not everyone liked Miss Marple. While Inspector Neele thought she was '*nice, very shrewd*', one murder suspect considered her to be '*an old hag*' and the vicar's wife regarded her as '*that terrible Miss Marple … the worst cat in the village … she knows every single thing that happens – and draws the worst inferences from it*'.

She was even considered '*dangerous*' by the vicar for all that he liked her and admired her sense of humour.

As well as the proclivities of her neighbours, Miss Marple also knew a thing or two about birds and gardening, creating in her own garden a Japanese area and a rockery; and she very much preferred flowers – especially peonies – to vegetables. It was a very sad day for her when, not least because of her arthritis and a rheumatic knee, the village doctor instructed her to stop stooping and kneeling, effectively bringing her gardening hobby to an end.

Inside Danemead, Miss Marple enjoyed home-baking – for her, fresh bread had '*the most delicious smell in the world*' and she loved plum tart. She also enjoyed making her own cowslip wine and plum brandy and also cherry brandy, made to her grandmother's recipe. However, while she was never an advocate of teetotalism, Miss Marple did have other Victorian sensibilities. She disliked bodily words like 'pregnant' and 'stomach'.

She was '*not entirely approving of unmarried motherhood*' and she was always quick to warn young women about the risk of '*unwise liaisons*'. And she also had a Victorian fear of foreigners, a trait that she herself considered to be quite absurd.

> '*A hundred years ago, you would certainly have been burned as a witch!*'
> Lucy Eyelesbarrow, *4.50 from Paddington*

Nonetheless, Miss Marple's cleverness and her strong sense of right and wrong were not lost on her family or any of her very wide circle of friends and acquaintances. It is therefore not surprising to learn that senior policemen and the Chief Constables of *several* counties also took Miss Marple very seriously, admiring her sharp eye for detail and her clear mind.

While she had resolved dozens of small, wholly unimportant village mysteries and even helped to unravel at least one earlier murder, her first 'really big' case was the killing of Colonel Lucius Protheroe, whose body was discovered in the vicarage at St Mary Mead.

'There is no detective in England equal to a spinster lady of uncertain age with plenty of time on her hands.'
Rev. Leonard Clement, *The Murder at the Vicarage*

And after this case, Miss Marple would go on to investigate murders in other villages and in the Caribbean and London, on holidays made possible by her indulgent nephew. And while she would prevent crimes from happening she would also resolve mysteries that were many decades old.

Shrewd, inspired and inspiring, Miss Marple was in short the '*complete detective service in the home*'.

And she always will be.

Tony Medawar

'She's just the finest detective God ever made. Natural genius cultivated in a suitable soil. She can tell you what might have happened and what ought to have happened and even what actually *did* happen! And she can tell you *why* it happened!'

---◆·---

Sir Henry Clithering
A Murder is Announced

1

THE ART OF
CONVERSATION

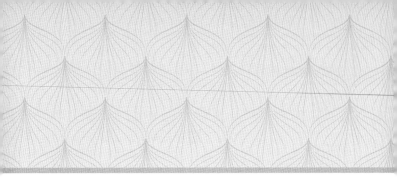

'If people do not choose to lower their voices, one must assume that they are prepared to be overheard.'

———— • ◆ • ————

At Bertram's Hotel

'Conversations are always dangerous,
if you have something to hide.'

A Caribbean Mystery

'Very nasty things go on in a village,
I assure you. … One has an opportunity
of studying things there that one
would never have in a town.'

———————•◆•———————

They Do It with Mirrors

'When we repeat a conversation, we don't, as a rule, repeat the actual words; we put in some other words that seem to us to mean exactly the same thing.'

'The Thumb Mark of St Peter'

'People aren't really foolish, you know.
Not in villages.'

The Mirror Crack'd from Side to Side

'The English *are* rather odd that way. Even in war, so much prouder of their defeats and their retreats than of their victories … we always seem to be almost embarrassed by a victory – and treat it as though it weren't quite nice to boast about it.'

———— • ◆ • ————

They Do It with Mirrors

'For an old lady like me who has all the time in the world, as you might say, it's really *expected* of her that there should be a great deal of unnecessary talk.'

———— • ◆ • ————

A Pocket Full of Rye

'I expect someone overheard something, though, don't you? ...
I mean, somebody always *does*.'

The Murder at the Vicarage

'It is never easy to repeat a conversation and be entirely accurate in what the other party has said. One is always inclined to jump at what you think they meant. Then, afterwards, you put actual words into their mouths.'

———— • ◆ • ————

A Caribbean Mystery

2

MEN & WOMEN

'We old women always do snoop.
It would be very odd and much
more noticeable if I didn't.'

A Murder is Announced

'Gentlemen, when they've had
a disappointment, want something
stronger than tea.'

The Mirror Crack'd from Side to Side

'So like men – quite unable to see
what's going on under their eyes.'

———————•◆•———————

4:50 from Paddington

'The kind of woman who finds it very hard to make herself believe that anything at all extraordinary or out of the way could happen. She's most unsuggestible, rather like granite.'

———— ◆ ————

4:50 from Paddington

'Women must stick together –
one should, in an emergency,
stand by one's own sex.'

———— • ◆ • ————

'The Affair at the Bungalow'

'There is no doubt about it that
husbands do, very frequently, want
to make away with their wives, though
sometimes, of course, they only *wish*
to make away with their wives
and do not actually do so.'

———— • ◆ • ————

The Mirror Crack'd from Side to Side

'Gentlemen … are frequently not as
level-headed as they seem.'

The Body in the Library

'Gentlemen never see through these things. And I'm afraid they often think we old women are – well, cats, to see things the way we do. But there it is. One does know a great deal about one's own sex, unfortunately.'

'The Four Suspects'

'I've known many cases where the most beautiful and ethereal girls have shown next to no moral scruple – though, of course, gentlemen never wish to believe it of them.'

————— ◆ —————

The Murder at the Vicarage

'Gentlemen always make such
excellent memoranda.'

———◆———

The Murder at the Vicarage

'If a man gets a formula that works –
he won't stop. He'll go on.'

A Caribbean Mystery

'A very nice woman. The kind that would so easily marry a bad lot. In fact, the sort of woman that would marry a murderer if she were ever given half a chance.'

Nemesis

'She's the kind of woman … that everyone likes. The kind of woman that could go on getting married again and again. I don't mean a *man's* woman – that's quite different.'

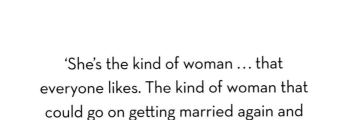

The Body in the Library

3

CRIME &
DETECTION

'The great thing in these cases is to keep an absolutely open mind. Most crimes, you see, are so absurdly simple.'

The Moving Finger

'Any coincidence … is *always* worth noticing. You can throw it away later if it *is* only a coincidence.'

—————— ◆ ——————

Nemesis

'When you only look at one side of a thing, you only see one side … But everything fits in perfectly well if you can only make up your mind what is reality and what is illusion.'

———————— ◆ ————————

They Do It with Mirrors

'It's like looking for a needle in a haystack. If you stick your fingers in it long enough, you ought to come up with something – even if one does get pricked in the process.'

Nemesis

'I know that in books it is always the most unlikely person. But I never find that rule applies in real life.'

— ◆ —

The Murder at the Vicarage

'If you disregard the smoke and come to the fire, you know where you are. You just come down to the actual facts of what happened.'

The Moving Finger

'I always find it prudent to suspect everyone just a little. What I say is, you really never *know*, do you?'

———— • ◆ • ————

The Murder at the Vicarage

'The common-sense explanation.
I've found, you know, that that is
so often right.'

———— • ◆ • ————

Sleeping Murder

'Money ... is a very powerful motive.'

———————•◆•———————

The Body in the Library

'You say crime goes unpunished;
but does it? Unpunished by the law
perhaps; but cause and effect works
outside the law. To say that every crime
brings its own punishment is by way
of being a platitude, and yet in my
opinion nothing can be truer.'

'The Four Suspects'

'From what I have heard and read, a man who does a wicked crime like this and gets away with it the first time, is, alas, *encouraged*. He thinks it's easy, he thinks he's clever. And so he repeats it.'

A Caribbean Mystery

'It is always the *obvious* person who
has done the crime.'

———— • ◆ • ————

The Mirror Crack'd from Side to Side

'There are many ways we prefer to look at things. But one must actually take facts as they are, must one not?'

—————•◆•—————

The Murder at the Vicarage

'Nemesis is long delayed sometimes,
but it comes in the end.'

Nemesis

'It's always interesting when one doesn't see ... If you don't see what a thing means you must be looking at it the wrong way round, unless of course you haven't got full information.'

———— ◆ ————

The Mirror Crack'd from Side to Side

'One must provide an explanation for everything. Each thing has got to be explained away satisfactorily. If you have a theory that fits every fact – well, then, it must be the right one.'

The Murder at the Vicarage

'It's not a question of what people have said. It's really a question of conjuring tricks.'

———— • ◆ • ————

They Do It with Mirrors

4

THE YOUNG

'One does need so much *tact*
when dealing with the young.'

———————— • ◆ • ————————

A Caribbean Mystery

'You wouldn't like my opinion, dear.
Young people never do, I notice.
It is better to say nothing.'

'Ingots of Gold'

'Children feel things, you know … They feel things more than the people around them ever imagine. The sense of hurt, of being rejected, of not belonging. It's a thing that you don't get over, just because of advantages.'

The Mirror Crack'd from Side to Side

'I remember a saying of my Great Aunt Fanny's. I was sixteen at the time and thought it particularly foolish. … She used to say: "The young people think the old people are fools; but the old people *know* the young people are fools."'

The Murder at the Vicarage

'If a young man had made up his mind to the great wickedness of taking a fellow creature's life, he would not appear distraught about it afterwards. It would be a premeditated and cold-blooded action.'

———— •◆• ————

The Murder at the Vicarage

'A young girl needs her mother's knowledge of the world and experience.'

———— ◆ ————

A Caribbean Mystery

'Life is more worth living, more full of interest when you are likely to lose it. It shouldn't be, perhaps, but it is. When you're young and strong and healthy, and life stretches ahead of you, living isn't really important at all … But old people know how valuable life is and how interesting.'

———— • ◆ • ————

A Caribbean Mystery

'Young men are so hot-headed and often prone to believe the worst.'

The Murder at the Vicarage

'None of these young people ever stop to *think*. They really don't examine the facts. Surely the whole crux of the matter is this: *How often is tittle tattle, as you call it, true!* And I think if, as I say, they really examined the facts they would find that it was true nine times out of ten!'

———— • ◆ • ————

'A Christmas Tragedy'

'Old people can be rather a nuisance, my dear. Newly married couples should be left to themselves.'

Sleeping Murder

'Clever young men know so little of life.'

———————◆ ◆ ◆———————

The Murder at the Vicarage

5

MURDER!

'Murders can happen anywhere …
and do.'

———— • ◆ • ————

The Mirror Crack'd from Side to Side

'Murderers always find it difficult to keep things simple. They can't keep themselves from elaborating.'

A Caribbean Mystery

'To commit a successful murder must be very much like bringing off a conjuring trick.'

The Moving Finger

'Many murderers have been delightful and pleasant men and people have been astonished. They are what I call the respectable killers. The ones who would commit murder for entirely utilitarian motives.'

———— • ◆ • ————

Nemesis

'To commit a murder, I think you need bravery – or perhaps, more often, just conceit.'

—————— ◆ ——————

They Do It with Mirrors

'Murders so often are quite simple –
with an obvious rather sordid motive.'

———————•◆•———————

4:50 from Paddington

'Murder – the wish to do murder – is
something quite different. It – how shall
I say? – it defies God.'

At Bertram's Hotel

'One is always inclined to guess – and guessing would be very wrong when it is a question of anything as serious as murder. All one can do is to observe the people concerned – or who might have been concerned – and see of whom they remind you.'

———— • ◆ • ————

4:50 from Paddington

'When anyone has committed one murder, they don't shrink from another, do they? Nor even from a third.'

The Body in the Library

'I dare say it has nothing to do with the murder. But it is a Peculiar Thing. And just at present we all feel we must take notice of Peculiar Things.'

———————— •◆• ————————

The Murder at the Vicarage

'Murder isn't a game.'

————————◆————————

A Murder is Announced

'The one thing I do know about murderers is that they can never let well alone. Or perhaps one should say – ill alone.'

4:50 from Paddington

'If they tried once, they'll try again.
If you've made up your mind to murder
someone you don't stop because the
first time it didn't come off. Especially if
you're not suspected.'

———————— • ◆ • ————————

A Murder is Announced

6

MISS MARPLE
ON MISS MARPLE

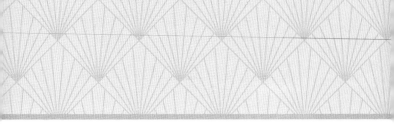

'I'm very ordinary. An ordinary rather scatty old lady. And that of course is very good *camouflage*.'

Nemesis

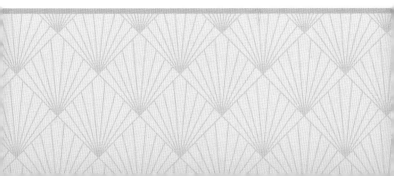

'Any little secret is quite safe with me.'

———————— • ◆ • ————————

The Murder at the Vicarage

'When one thinks of things just before
going to sleep, quite often ideas come.'

Nemesis

'I am a noticing kind of person.'

The Murder at the Vicarage

'If I get stories told to me rather often,
I don't really mind hearing them again
because I've usually forgotten them.'

———————— • ◆ • ————————

A Caribbean Mystery

'If you expect me to feel sympathy, regret, urge an unhappy childhood, blame bad environment; if you expect me to weep over him, this young murderer of yours, I do not feel inclined to do so. I do not like evil beings who do evil things.'

Nemesis

'I've never been an advocate of teetotalism. A little strong drink is always advisable on the premises in case there is a shock or an accident. Invaluable at such times. Or, of course, if a gentleman should arrive suddenly.'

———— • ◆ • ————

The Mirror Crack'd from Side to Side

'There's no point in saving at my age.'

Nemesis

'I'm afraid I am *rather* romantic. Because
I am an old maid, perhaps.'

———— • ◆ • ————

4:50 from Paddington

'One is alone when the last one
who *remembers* is gone.'

———————— • ◆ • ————————

A Murder is Announced

'My nephew Raymond tells me (in fun, of course and quite affectionately) that I have a mind like a *sink*. He says that most Victorians have. All I can say is that the Victorians knew a good deal about human nature.'

The Body in the Library

'My hobby is – and always has been –
Human Nature.'

———— • ◆ • ————

The Murder at the Vicarage

'It is true, of course, that I have lived what is called a very uneventful life, but I have had a lot of experiences in solving different little problems that have arisen. Some of them have been really quite ingenious, but it would be no good telling them to you, because they are about such unimportant things that you would not be interested.'

———— • ◆ • ————

'The Thumb Mark of St Peter'

'I always believe the worst.
What is so sad is that one is
usually justified in doing so.'

A Pocket Full of Rye

'*I* look every minute of *my* age.'

They Do It with Mirrors

'I don't know why you should assume
that I think of murder *all* the time.'

—— • ◆ • ——

The Mirror Crack'd from Side to Side

'I have no gifts – no gifts at all – except perhaps a certain knowledge of human nature. People, I find, are apt to be far too trustful. I'm afraid that I have a tendency always to believe the worst. Not a nice trait. But so often justified by subsequent events.'

A Murder is Announced

'I take an interest in everything.'

———————— • ◆ • ————————

The Mirror Crack'd from Side to Side

'When I am in really bad trouble
I always say a little prayer to myself –
anywhere, when I am walking along
the street, or at a bazaar. And
I always get an answer.'

———————— ◆ ————————

'The Thumb Mark of St Peter'

7

---•◆•---

HUMAN NATURE

'So many people seem to me not to be either bad nor good but, simply, you know, very silly.'

'The Tuesday Night Club'

'People's memories are very short –
a lucky thing, I always think.'

———————— • ◆ • ————————

'The Thumb Mark of St Peter'

'The most nervous people are far more brave than one really thinks they are.'

————— • ◆ • —————

'The Blue Geranium'

'A lot of people are stupid. And
stupid people get found out, whatever
they do. But there are quite a number
of people who aren't stupid, and one
shudders to think of what they might
accomplish unless they had very
strongly rooted principles.'

———————•◆•———————

'The Four Suspects'

'There's such a thing as a secret
inside a secret.'

'Strange Jest'

'Everybody is very much alike, really.
But fortunately, perhaps,
they don't realise it.'

'The Thumb Mark of St Peter'

'There is nothing you can tell me about people's minds that would astonish or surprise me.'

---◆---

'The Thumb Mark of St Peter'

'Most people – and I don't exclude policemen – are far too trusting for this wicked world. They believe what is told them. I never do. I'm afraid I always like to prove a thing for myself.'

The Body in the Library

'The trouble is … that people are greedy. Some people. That's so often, you know, how things start. You don't start with murder, with wanting to do murder, or even thinking of it. You just start by being greedy, by wanting more than you're going to have.'

———— • ◆ • ————

4:50 from Paddington

'It's just perseverance, isn't it,
that leads to things.'

———————— • ◆ • ————————

Nemesis

'Observing human nature for as long as I have done, one gets not to expect very much from it. I dare say the idle tittle-tattle is very wrong and unkind, but it is so often true, isn't it?'

———————— • ◆ • ————————

The Murder at the Vicarage

'People with a grudge against the world are always dangerous. They seem to think life owes them something.'

***

A Murder is Announced

'So many people are a little queer, aren't they? – in fact most people are when you know them well. And normal people do such astonishing things sometimes, and abnormal people are sometimes so very sane and ordinary.'

———— • ◆ • ————

The Murder at the Vicarage

'Weak and kindly people are often very treacherous. And if they've got a grudge against life it saps the little moral strength that they may possess.'

A Murder is Announced

'People are highly credulous … they believe what they are told … We're all inclined to do that.'

———— ◆ ————

A Caribbean Mystery

'Whenever there is a question of *gain*, one has to be *very suspicious*. The great thing is to avoid having in any way a trustful mind.'

---·◆·---

A Pocket Full of Rye

'Human beings are so much
more vulnerable and sensitive
than anyone thinks.'

The Body in the Library

'Most people ... have a sense
of protection. They realise when it's
unwise to say or do something because
of the person or persons who are taking
in what you say, and because of the kind
of character that those people have.'

The Mirror Crack'd from Side to Side

'The depravity of human nature is unbelievable.'

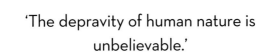

'Strange Jest'

'It really is very dangerous to believe people. *I* never have for years.'

———————— •◆• ————————

Sleeping Murder

'Cleverness isn't everything.'

———————•◆•———————

A Murder is Announced

8

LIFE

'Life is really a One Way Street, isn't it?'

At Bertram's Hotel

'Human nature is much the same
in a village as everywhere, only one has
opportunities and leisure for seeing
it at closer quarters.'

———— ◆ ————

'The Companion'

'It's not *impossible*, my dear. It's just a
very remarkable coincidence – and
remarkable coincidences do happen.'

Sleeping Murder

'One never can be quite sure about anyone, can one? At least that's what I've found.'

The Murder at the Vicarage

'It's important, you know, that
wickedness shouldn't triumph.'

———— • ◆ • ————

A Pocket Full of Rye

'One so often looks at a thing
the wrong way round.'

—— • ◆ • ——

'Greenshaw's Folly'

'The children of Lucifer are often beautiful – And as we know, they "flourish like the green bay tree".'

At Bertram's Hotel

'I have had too much experience of life to believe in the infallibility of doctors. Some of them are clever men and some of them are not, and half the time the best of them don't know what is the matter with you.'

'The Thumb Mark of St Peter'

'One cannot go through life
without attracting certain risks
if they are necessary.'

Nemesis

'The worst is so often true.'

———◆———

They Do It with Mirrors

'I always find one thing very like
another in this world.'

———————— ◆ ————————

'The Blood-Stained Pavement'

'Money … can do a lot to ease
one's path through life.'

<hr />

A Murder is Announced

'The way to a cook's heart, as they say,
is through her pastry.'

———————— • ◆ • ————————

A Pocket Full of Rye

'I am so old that death doesn't shock
me as much as it does you.'

———————— •◆• ————————

Sleeping Murder

'One needs a great deal of courage
to get through life.'

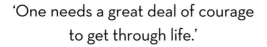

A Pocket Full of Rye

DOES A WOMAN'S INSTINCT MAKE HER A GOOD DETECTIVE?

by Agatha Christie

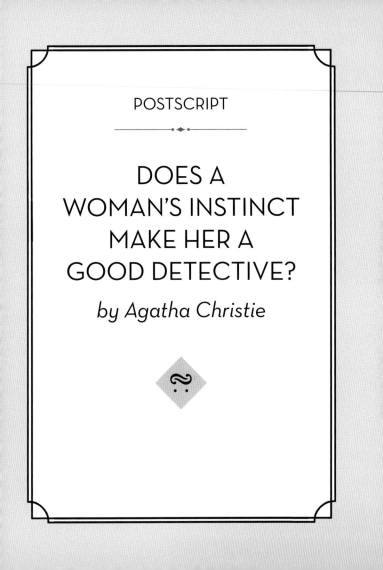

'Does a Woman's Instinct Make Her a Good Detective?' was first published on 14 May 1928 in *The Star*, a British newspaper, to coincide with the publication of the final story in the first set of six Miss Marple short stories in the *Royal* magazine.

A 'woman's instinct' is in any case a very debatable thing. We use the phrase glibly enough, but when we really come down to facts, what, after all, does it mean? Shorn of all glamour, I think it comes down to this – women prefer short cuts! They prefer the inspired guess to the more laborious process of solid reasoning. And, of course, the inspired guess is often right.

What kudos then for Mrs Smith! 'How could you tell, my dear?' says Mr Smith admiringly. And Mrs Smith answers negligently: 'I couldn't say. I just knew.'

But very intoxicating for Mrs Smith. To take no trouble at all, just make a leap in the dark and find it right! So, at Monte Carlo, we stake on a single number, and up it comes, and we say: 'Funny! I just knew seven was coming up that time!' But what about the other times when we staked on eight and nine and ten, and they didn't turn up? Well, we don't talk about them. Just as Mr Smith, returning from the City, talks a good deal about the coup he made in tin, how by far-seeing reasoning he deduced that tin was going to be a 'good thing'. But he doesn't mention the cropper he came over lead where his reasoning proved to be faulty.

There is this to be said for Mr Smith's method. It may be slow, but it usually gets there in the end, and if it does not get there, it still gets somewhere not very far away. Mrs Smith may be magnificently right – but if not she is wildly wrong. And when we come to the tracking down of the criminal that is an important point to take into consideration.

Most criminals are caught in the end by patient methodical tracking down. Women are not methodical; they are tidy quite often, but methodical – no. Very few women are good housekeepers even while they have nothing else to do. On the other hand they are marvellously useful about the house. They can make something out of nothing, they can create an effect with the poorest material, they can hang pictures nearly as straight in half an hour as it would take Mr Smith a whole day with a foot rule and a spirit level! They have all sorts of odds and ends of information which would be invaluable to a tracker down of crime, but it is doubtful if they could use this knowledge to any effect themselves.

Because, after all, women are not really interested in crime. The criminal, when all is said and done, is just this – an enemy of society, and women do not really care about anything so impersonal as that. If a man has acquired a plethora of wives, or murdered his spouse for the sake of another, they are interested. It is the personal side that attracts them.

They lack, too, the spirit of the chase. Men love hunting things – whether foxes or other men. They do not mind if the chase is active or passive. They will stay on the banks of a stream in the rain for hours in the hopes of circumventing and capturing an elusive fish!

Women lack this instinct of the chase. When a convict escapes, women say: 'Poor fellow, I hope he won't be caught.' The fact that, for the sake of the community, the man would be better behind bolts and bars leaves them cold. If anyone attacks their own man or children, that is a different matter. Women are relentless when really aroused. But the embezzling of bank funds hardly stirs them to interest.

Yet in a private and personal capacity women are wonderful detectives. They know all about Mr Jones and Miss Brown, and that the Robinsons aren't getting on so well as they did, and that Mr White married Mrs White for her money. There is no deceiving them. They just know!

Because, you see, they are interested. The Whites live next door, and the Robinsons just over the way. And that is what matters in this life.

It was probably just the same in the Stone Age. Mr Ooly Boohgah went off over the heather with his club to do a little agreeable killing, and Mrs Ooly Boohgah looked into the next 'hut' circle and saw that Mrs Og Bog was wearing a new set of skins and wondered where she got them. And after thinking a minute or two, she knew! The pity of it was that Mr Ooly Boohgah wasn't a bit interested. Men never are!

Agatha Christie

MISS MARPLE'S CASEBOOK

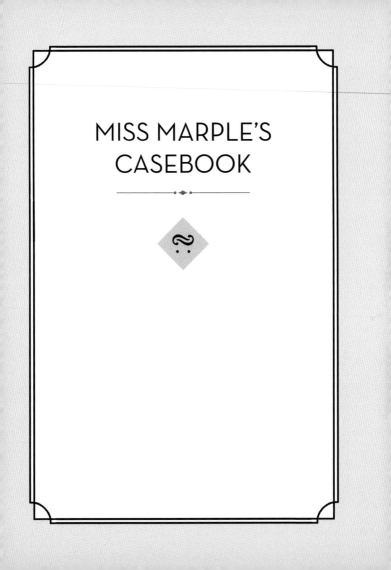

'I so often seem to get mixed up in the things that are really *no* concern of mine. Crimes I mean, and peculiar happenings.'

———— ◆ • ————

A Pocket Full of Rye

MISS MARPLE: THE NOVELS

The twelve Miss Marple novels were originally published in the UK by Collins Crime Club (London), and in the US by Dodd, Mead & Co. (New York).

The Murder at the Vicarage (1930)
The Body in the Library (1942)
The Moving Finger (US 1942, UK 1943)
A Murder is Announced (1950)
They Do It with Mirrors (1952)
A Pocket Full of Rye (UK 1953, US 1954)
4.50 from Paddington (1957)
The Mirror Crack'd from Side to Side (UK 1962, US 1963 as *The Mirror Crack'd*)
A Caribbean Mystery (UK 1964, US 1965)
At Bertram's Hotel (UK 1965, US 1966)
Nemesis (1971)
Sleeping Murder (1976. This novel was written in the 1940s and saved for publication until after Agatha Christie died.)

MISS MARPLE: THE SHORT STORIES

This bibliography gives the first publication of each story anywhere in the world.

'The Tuesday Night Club' (*The Royal Magazine*, December 1927)

'The Idol House of Astarte' (*The Royal Magazine*, January 1928)

'Ingots of Gold' (*The Royal Magazine*, February 1928)

'The Bloodstained Pavement' (*The Royal Magazine*, March 1928)

'Motive v Opportunity' (*The Royal Magazine*, April 1928)

'The Thumb Mark of St Peter' (*The Royal Magazine*, May 1928)

'The Blue Geranium' (*The Story-Teller Magazine*, December 1929)

'The Four Suspects' (*Pictorial Review*, January 1930)

'A Christmas Tragedy' (*The Story-Teller Magazine*, January 1930, as 'The Hat and the Alibi')

'The Companion' (*The Story-Teller Magazine*, February 1930, as 'The Resurrection of Amy Durrant')

'The Herb of Death' (*The Story-Teller Magazine*, March 1930)

'The Affair at the Bungalow' (*The Story-Teller Magazine*, May 1930)

'Death by Drowning (*Nash's Pall Mall Magazine*, November 1931)

'Miss Marple Tells a Story' (*Home Journal*, 25 May 1935, as 'Behind Closed Doors'. First broadcast on radio, on the BBC National Programme, on 11 May 1934, when the story was read by Agatha Christie.)

'Strange Jest' (*This Week Magazine*, 2 November 1941)

'Tape-Measure Murder' (*This Week Magazine*, 16 November 1941)

'The Case of the Caretaker' (*Strand Magazine*, January 1942. An earlier draft, 'The Case of the Caretaker's Wife', was published in *Agatha Christie's Murder in the Making* by John Curran, 1 September 2011.)

'The Case of the Perfect Maid' (*Strand Magazine*, April 1942, as 'The Perfect Maid')

'Sanctuary' (*This Week Magazine*, 12 and 19 September 1954, as 'Murder at the Vicarage')

'Greenshaw's Folly' (*Star Weekly*, August 1956)